FRANKENSTEIN

MARY WOLLSTONECRAFT SHELLEY

Condensed and Adapted by
BETHANY SNYDER

Illustrated by
MIRACLE STUDIOS

bendon

The Junior Classics have been
adapted and illustrated with care and thought
to introduce you to a world of famous authors, characters, ideas,
and great stories that have been loved for generations.

Editor — Kathryn Knight
Creative Director — Gina Rhodes Haynes
And the entire classics project team

FRANKENSTEIN

Copyright © 2014 Bendon
Ashland, Ohio 44805 • 1-888-5-BENDON
bendonpub.com

Cover design by Mary Katherine Ethridge

Printed in the United States of America

A *note to the reader*—

A classic story rests in your hands. The characters are famous. The tale is timeless.

This Junior Classic edition of *Frankenstein* has been carefully condensed and adapted from the original version (which you really *must* read when you're ready for every detail). We kept the well-known phrases for you. We kept Mary Shelley's style. And we kept the important imagery and heart of the tale.

Literature is terrific fun! It encourages you to think. It helps you dream. It is full of heroes and villains, suspense and humor, adventure and wonder, and new ideas. It introduces you to writers who reach out across time to say: "Do you want to hear a story I wrote?"

Curl up and enjoy.

CONTENTS

CHARACTERS

CAPTAIN ROBERT WALTON — a young man who undertakes a heroic voyage to find the North Pole, and finds instead Victor Frankenstein on the ice

MRS. MARGARET SAVILLE — the captain's sister, to whom he writes all his letters

VICTOR FRANKENSTEIN — a young man with grand ideas who creates a living man from body parts

MR. and MRS. ALPHONSE FRANKENSTEIN — Victor's wealthy parents

ELIZABETH LAVENZA — the abandoned girl the Frankensteins adopt, who loves Victor and becomes his bride

ERNEST — Victor's brother, seven years younger

WILLIAM — Victor's youngest brother, who is mysteriously murdered

HENRY CLERVAL — Victor's best friend, who joins him at the university

CHARACTERS

PROFESSOR KREMPE — the physics teacher who tells Victor that his alchemy studies are nonsense

PROFESSOR WALDMAN — the chemistry teacher who encourages Victor to study the secrets of nature

THE MONSTER — the man created by Victor, who fends for himself and vows revenge against his creator

JUSTINE MORITZ — housekeeper for the Frankenstein family, who is charged with young William's murder

MR. DeLACEY — the blind, old cottager, who keeps up his poor family's spirits by playing the guitar

AGATHA DeLACEY — Mr. DeLacey's daughter

FELIX DeLACEY — Mr. DeLacey's son

SAFIE — a young Turkish lady, who finds her beloved Felix at the cottage

MR. KIRWIN — the kindly judge in Scotland

FRANKENSTEIN

CHAPTER ONE

Captain Walton's Letters

To Mrs. Saville, England
St. Petersburg, Russia, Dec. 11th

I am already far north of London. I enjoy walking in the streets of Petersburg. I feel a cold northern breeze play upon my cheeks. It both chills me and fills me with delight. My daydreams about reaching the North Pole are now more exciting and clear.

I do not believe that the North Pole is a place of frost and emptiness. I believe it is a place of beauty and delight. Think of the wonders that await me! I will see a part of the world that has never been visited before, and walk upon a land

that has never been touched by man. I am so excited that I have no fear of danger or death. I feel only joy, like a child feels when he sets out in a little boat with his friends on a stream. To think, dear sister, that I will be the first man to discover a route to the North Pacific Ocean! What knowledge I'll bring to mankind!

Six years have passed since I decided to make this journey. It has been a dream of mine since I was very young. And now, dear Margaret, do I not deserve to accomplish some great purpose? I could have spent my life in luxury, but I prefer glory instead of wealth.

I will leave for the northern town of Archangel in two or three weeks. I do not intend to sail for the North Pole until the month of June. When will I return? Ah, dear sister, how can I answer this question? If I succeed, many months—perhaps years—will pass before you and I may meet again. If I fail, you will see me again soon… or never.

Farewell, my dear Margaret. May heaven shower blessings upon you.

Your loving brother,
R. Walton

To Mrs. Saville, England
Archangel, March 28th

The time passes slowly here, where we are surrounded by frost and snow! I have hired a ship and am busy hiring sailors. But I am lonely. I have no true friend here—no one who is courageous, intelligent, and whose tastes are like my own. Well, these are useless complaints. I will find no friend on the wide ocean.

I will leave as soon as the weather improves. The winter has been terrible, but spring is expected to come early. I may sail sooner than I had hoped.

I love you very much. If you never hear from me again, think of me with affection.

Your loving brother,
Robert Walton

To Mrs. Saville, England
July 7th

My dear Sister,

I am safe and have made progress on my voyage. We have already sailed to the icy north. It is the middle of summer, but of course it is not as warm as it is in England.

Good-bye, my dear Margaret. I will be careful, I promise you. But I *will* be successful. Why not? Nothing can stop the determined will of man.

May heaven bless you!

R.W.

To Mrs. Saville, England
August 5th

A very strange accident has happened to us. Last Monday we were almost surrounded by ice and a very thick fog. This was far too dangerous for travel, so we stopped the ship, hoping for a change in the weather.

About two o'clock the mist cleared away. All around us we saw great sheets of ice that seemed to have no end. Some of the sailors groaned. Even I began to worry. Suddenly we saw a strange sight! A sled pulled by dogs was moving towards the north about a half a mile from our ship. A thing which was shaped like a man—but gigantic in size—guided the dogs. We watched the traveler with our telescopes for some time.

This filled us with wonder, since we were many hundred miles from any land. We wanted to follow him, but we were shut in by the ice.

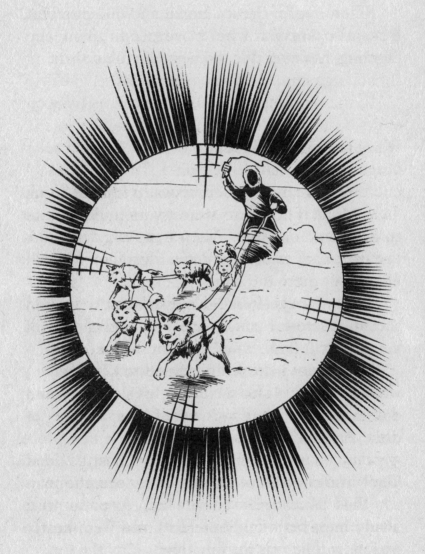

Before night, the ice broke and our ship was free. We stayed where we were until the morning, however. We did not want to risk hitting those large chunks of ice in the dark.

In the morning I found all the sailors busy on one side of the ship, talking to someone in the sea. There was a sled, like the one we had seen before, which had drifted on a slab of ice. Only one dog was alive. But there was a human being on the sled. The sailors were trying to get him to come aboard our ship. When I appeared on deck the first mate said, "Here is our captain. He will not allow you to die on the open sea."

The stranger spoke English with a foreign accent. "Before I come on board," he said, "will you kindly tell me where you are headed?"

I could not believe he needed to know where we were going! If he stayed on his sled he would die! I replied that we were on a voyage of discovery towards the North Pole.

The man agreed to come on board. Good God! Margaret, if you could have seen the man who had almost refused our help, your surprise would have been endless. His limbs were nearly frozen, and he was terribly thin.

I took him to my cabin to care for him. Two days passed before he was able to speak.

I've never seen a more interesting man. His eyes seem wild and sometimes crazed. But if anyone is kind to him, his whole face lights up. Most often he is depressed and miserable.

When my lieutenant asked him why he had come so far on the ice, he instantly seemed sad. He replied, "To seek one who fled from me."

"Did this man travel in the same way?"

"Yes."

"Then I believe we have seen him," said the lieutenant. "The day before we picked you up we saw some dogs pulling a sled with a man in it."

The stranger became very excited. He asked questions about the route which the demon (as he called him) had taken. Later he said to me, "I know I have made you curious."

"Of course," I said. "But it would be very rude to trouble you with any questions of mine."

He asked if I thought the breaking up of the ice had destroyed the other sled. I replied that the ice had not broken until near midnight and that the traveler might have reached a safe place before that time.

Since then, the stranger has been filled with a new spirit of life. He wants to be on deck to watch for the other sled. But he is far too weak for this. I have promised that someone will let him know immediately if any new object appears.

I said in one of my letters that I would not find a friend on the ocean. Now I have found a man whom I would be happy to call my friend.

August 13th

My guest has recovered from his illness. He is constantly on the deck, watching for the other sled. We often talk about my dreams and goals. I told him that I would give up my money and my life to complete this voyage. I told him I believe that one man's life is a small price to pay for knowledge and power.

"Unhappy man!" the stranger said in horror. "Do you share my madness? Have you drunk of the same poison? Let me share my tale with you. You will knock that cup from your lips!" But he was weak from this outburst and could not go on.

Later he said, "Ah, but we *are* different. You have hope and the world before you. But I—I have lost everything and cannot begin life anew."

August 19th

Yesterday the stranger said to me, "I had decided that my memories should die with me. But you have convinced me to change my mind, Captain Walton. I see that you are about to suffer the same dangers. I think that you may learn a lesson from my tale. It may help you if you succeed on your voyage. Or it may comfort you if you fail. Prepare to hear about strange events."

He then told me that he would begin his story the next day. I have decided, dear Margaret, to write down in the evenings what he has told me during the day. I am sure that this manuscript will give you great pleasure. And I will read it with great interest on some future day.

How strange and disturbing must be his story! How frightful must be the storm that has tossed his soul—that gallant ship—and wrecked it so!

CHAPTER TWO

Frankenstein's Story Begins

My name is Victor Frankenstein. My family is from Geneva, Switzerland, where my father was a respected government official. My parents moved to Italy for a few years after they married. I, the eldest, was born in Naples.

When I was about five years old, we spent a week at Lake Como in Northern Italy. My mother always liked to help people in need. One day my mother and I visited a poor cottage. A peasant and his wife lived there with five hungry children. One of the five did not look like the others—she was much more fair and thin. Her hair was the brightest gold. She had clear blue eyes. Her lips and the shape of her face were sweet. She seemed almost heaven-sent.

The peasant woman explained that the little girl was not her own child, but an orphan. Her father was a wealthy Italian. No one knew where he was, or even if he was still alive. Her mother, who had died during childbirth, was German. The poor child had become a beggar. The peasants had taken her into their humble cottage, where she had bloomed like a rose.

When my father came home, he was surprised to find me playing with the little girl. With his permission, my mother asked to adopt her. The peasants knew she would have a better life with my family. And so, Elizabeth Lavenza became a member of my parents' house.

I was glad that everyone loved Elizabeth. On the evening before she was brought to my home, my mother said playfully, "I have a pretty present for my Victor. Tomorrow he will have it."

When she presented Elizabeth to me, I took her words very seriously. Elizabeth was mine to protect, love, and treasure. Until death she was to be mine only.

We were brought up together, for we were only a year apart. We had different natures, but we loved each other. Elizabeth was calmer than I was. She loved to read poetry. She loved the shapes of the mountains and the changes of the seasons. She was happy just to enjoy life. I wanted to know what caused life—the how and why of everything. To me the world was a secret to be discovered. I wanted to uncover the hidden laws of nature.

When I was seven, my brother Ernest was born and we settled in Switzerland, our home country. We owned a house in Geneva, but we lived mainly in a country estate on Lake Belrive. It was located about three miles from Geneva.

My best friend was Henry Clerval, the son of a businessman. He loved adventure, hard work, and even danger. He would tell me of books he'd read about bravery and romance. He wrote songs and stories about knightly adventures.

Two important things happened during my childhood that put me on the road to destruction. The first happened when I was thirteen. We all went on vacation to France. At an inn there I found a book about alchemy. This is the name of an ancient science. Alchemists believed it was possible to make people live forever. They also believed that they could bring people back from the dead. This book fascinated me.

I told my father about the book, but he called it "sad trash." I did not know then that modern science had proven these theories wrong. No one believed you could bring people back from the dead. But my father didn't explain these things. I found more books by other alchemists and read them all with wonder and delight.

My studies gave me many great ideas. What if I could prevent the human body from becoming sick? What if I could make people safe from death? And these were not my only dreams. I dreamed of contacting ghosts or devils. The alchemists believed it was possible.

The second thing that changed the course of my life happened when I was about fifteen. We were at our house in Belrive, and, as it happened,

a scientist was staying there with us. One night there was a violent thunderstorm. I watched the storm from the door as a bolt of lightning struck a tree near the house and burst into flames. The next morning we went to look at the tree. It wasn't splintered—it had almost *exploded!* All that was left were thin ribbons of wood. The scientist explained to me about the power of electricity. This man's theories made me even more curious and gave me fantastic ideas!

It was also about this time that a wonderful event blessed my family. My mother gave birth to another son, who was named William.

When I was seventeen my parents decided that I should go to the University of Ingolstadt in Germany. But before I could go, the first great sadness came to my life. It was a sign of my future misery.

Elizabeth had caught scarlet fever, and was close to death. My mother wanted to be the one to nurse Elizabeth back to health. When we told her it was too dangerous, she did not listen. Elizabeth got well again, but three days later my mother was ill. She did not recover. We mourned my mother's death for quite a long time.

Finally the time came for me to leave for the university. Henry spent the last evening with us. His father would not let him attend school with me. We stayed up late like young schoolboys, not wanting to say the word "Farewell."

The next day I sadly left my home. I promised my dear Elizabeth that I would write often.

CHAPTER THREE

My Studies

At the university, I first met Professor Krempe, who taught physics. He was a short, stout man with a gruff voice and a disgusting face. But he knew a great deal of the secrets of his science. He asked me about my own education. I mentioned the names of the alchemists I had studied.

"Have you really wasted your time studying that?" he demanded.

I replied that I had.

"Then all that time is lost," he bellowed. "Good God! My dear sir, you must begin your studies again from the start." He wrote down a list of several books on physics for me to read.

Professor Waldman taught chemistry. He was not like Professor Krempe at all. He had good posture, and he was a thoughtful, kind man. He talked about modern chemistry with a mellow voice. I will never forget what he said:

"Modern scientists have performed miracles. They dig into the hiding places of nature. They uncover how nature works."

I was fascinated by the professor's words. "So much has been done by scientists," I said to myself, "but *I* will achieve even more! I will explore unknown powers. I will reveal to mankind the deepest mysteries of the world."

Professor Waldman did not laugh when I told him I had been reading about the alchemists. He called them "men of genius."

He then took me into his laboratory and explained to me the uses of the many machines. He also gave me a list of books to read about modern chemistry. I will never forget that day. It decided my future destiny.

I became very involved in my studies. Professor Waldman became my good friend, and he helped me set up my own laboratory. There I often stayed up all night working.

Two years passed. During this time, I wrote to Elizabeth and my family, but I did not visit Geneva. I worked so hard that at the end of two years I made improvements to some chemical instruments. This brought me great respect at the university. I knew as much about physics as any professor. There was not much more that I could learn there, so I could have gone home. But listen to my tale, and you will know why I did not.

I had become interested in the life that streams through the human body. Where did it come from? It was a brave question. I wanted to discover the answer. I decided to focus on the branches of science that relate to the body.

I needed to see how the human body changed after death. Darkness and graveyards did not scare me, and I began to visit tombs and morgues. I studied the bodies and noted all the changes after death. I had ideas on how the body goes from life to death, and then… from death to life.

In this darkness a sudden light came upon me. It was a brilliant, wonderful, simple idea. Was I truly the first to discover it? I had stumbled upon the cause of life. No, it was something more. I had discovered how *I* could bring something to life!

I see by the look in your eyes, Captain Walton, that you want to know my secret. That cannot be. Listen patiently until the end of my story. You will see why I cannot tell you. You will see how dangerous knowledge can be.

I knew that an amazing power was placed in my hands. Should I actually create something and bring it to life? Should I put together the parts... of a human being? I would need muscles, veins, bones. Think of what I would add to science! Think of the glory! I knew I must do it!

And so I began the creation of a human being. I decided to make the creature gigantic in size— eight feet tall—to make the smaller parts easier to work with. I was enthusiastic with my work. Oh, think of the happy creatures that would owe their lives to me! I would be their father.

As I worked, I grew pale and weak. I could think of nothing else. I failed many times, but tried again. Can you imagine the horrors of my secret work? I hunted through fresh graves. I collected bones from morgues. Thinking about it now makes my body tremble and my eyes water. But then I was desperate to finish my work. I did not care how gruesome it was.

My workshop was in a private room at the top of the house. It was separated from the other apartments by a hall and a staircase. I worked so hard that my eyeballs stared from their sockets. I was often disgusted by my work, but I could not stop.

The summer months passed. It was a beautiful season, but my eyes were blind to nature. I kept working with all my heart and soul. I also forgot the family that I had not seen for such a long time. I knew my silence troubled them, but I could not stop working. Surely my father and Elizabeth wondered about me. Winter, spring, and summer passed.

I know now that a person should always keep a calm, peaceful mind—and not become crazed with work. If you study something day and night and forget the simple things in life, you cannot be happy. If you work at something so long and hard that it makes you forget those you love, then that work is not good. Oh, think how much better life would be if we did not strive after glory, Captain Walton. Ah, but I'm giving you a lesson during the most interesting part of my tale, yes? Your looks remind me to go on.

That whole year, I never watched blossoms open or leaves change. I was too excited about my work. But I also spent time worrying. Every night I went to bed with a fever. I became nervous and jumpy. The fall of a leaf would startle me. I stayed away from the other students, as if I were guilty of a crime. Sometimes I became alarmed at how awful I looked. But I knew that my work would soon come to an end. I promised myself that I would exercise and have fun when my creation was complete.

CHAPTER FOUR

It Breathed!

It was on a dreary night in November that I finished. I readied the tool to put a spark of life into the thing that lay at my feet. It was already one in the morning. The rain pattered against the windows. My candle was nearly burnt out.

Then I saw the dull yellow eye of the creature open. It breathed hard. Its limbs shook.

How can I describe the monster? I had made sure that his limbs were all the same size. I had chosen a beautiful face for him. Beautiful?! Great God! His shriveled, yellow skin hardly covered the muscles and arteries. His eyes and eye sockets were brownish-white. He had straight black lips.

I had worked hard for nearly two years to bring a creature to life. I had denied myself rest and health. Now that I was finished, the beauty of my dream vanished. Horror and disgust filled my heart. I could not look at the face, and I rushed out of the room!

I ran to my bedroom, where I walked back and forth trying to calm my mind. I was exhausted. I threw myself onto my bed, trying to forget what I had done. I did fall asleep, but I had terrible nightmares about death.

I awoke in horror. A cold sweat covered my forehead. My teeth chattered, and every limb shook. Then, by the dim yellow light of the moon, I saw the monster force its way into the room. His eyes stared at me. His jaws opened and he muttered some strange sounds. A grin wrinkled his cheeks. One hand was stretched out as if to stop me, but I escaped and rushed downstairs. I spent the rest of the night in the courtyard of the house, walking around in the greatest panic.

In the morning I left the courtyard and went into the streets. I did not dare return to the apartment. I was drenched by the rain which poured from the black sky, but I did not stop.

Finally I reached the inn where the carriages usually stopped. I saw the stagecoach from Switzerland coming towards me. It stopped just where I was standing. As the door opened, I saw Henry Clerval jump out.

"Victor!" he exclaimed. "I am so glad to see you! How lucky that you are here!"

Clerval! When I saw him, I thought of Father and Elizabeth and my home. In a moment, I forgot my horror. For the first time in many months I felt a peaceful joy. Henry told me that his father had finally agreed to let him come to the university.

"I am delighted to see you," I said. "But tell me how my father, brothers, and Elizabeth are."

"Very well. Although it makes them nervous that you never write or visit. But, Victor," he continued, looking at my face, "how very ill you look. So thin and pale! You look as if you have not slept for several nights."

"You are right. I have been so busy that I have not allowed myself enough rest. But I hope—oh, how I hope—that I am now free."

I could not bear to think about the night before. I could never tell Henry what had happened!

Before long, we had walked to the college and my own apartment door. What if the creature was still in there! I did not want to see the monster, but I feared even more that Henry might see him. I asked my friend to wait for a few minutes. Then I ran up to my rooms.

A cold shivering came over me. I threw the door open quickly. Nothing appeared. I stepped in fearfully. No creature. I checked my bedroom. No hideous guest. I could hardly believe my good luck. The monster had fled! I clapped my hands for joy and ran down to get Henry.

We went up to my place and had breakfast. I was so happy that I jumped over the chairs, clapped my hands, and laughed out loud. My strange behavior frightened and confused Henry.

Suddenly I fell down unconscious. This was the beginning of a fever which tortured me for several months. Henry was my only nurse. I learned that during the whole time he did not tell my family how serious my illness was.

While I was sick I imagined that the monster was in the room with me. I remember, as if in a daze, that I talked about him constantly. I am sure my words surprised Henry.

I recovered very slowly. When I began to be in my own mind again, I realized that it was already spring. My gloom disappeared and I felt joy.

"My good friend Clerval," I said, "how kind, how very good you are to me. You must have missed school this whole winter taking care of me. How can I repay you?"

"Repay me by getting well," Clerval said. "Since you're feeling better, may I speak to you about one subject?"

I trembled. One subject! What could it be? Could it be that I talked about...! I trembled more.

"Calm down," said Clerval. "I just thought your father and Elizabeth would be glad to get a letter from you in your own handwriting."

"Is that all, Henry? Of course I will write."

"Ah, then you would like to read this letter. It's been here for a few days. It's from Elizabeth."

Clerval put the letter into my hands.

CHAPTER FIVE

I Begin My Life Again

My dearest Victor,

Henry writes that you are getting better. I hope that we will soon have a letter from you saying it is true. Get well—and return to us. You will find a cheerful home and friends who love you dearly.

Your father is in good health. He asks only to see you and to know that you are well. How pleased you would be to see your brother Ernest! He is now sixteen and full of spirit. His time is spent climbing the hills or rowing on the lake.

And our little darling William! I wish you could see him, Victor. He is very tall for his age, with sweet laughing blue eyes, dark eyelashes, and

curling hair. His cheeks are rosy with health.

Justine Moritz, our housekeeper and dear friend, has been through a tragedy. Her mother died last winter. But Justine has since returned to us. I love her tenderly. She constantly reminds me of your dear mother.

Write, dearest Victor. One word will be a blessing to us. Ten thousand thanks to Henry for his kindness and his many letters. Farewell! Take care of yourself, and, I beg you, write!

Elizabeth Lavenza
Geneva, March 18th

"Dear, dear Elizabeth!" I exclaimed when I had read her letter. "I will write instantly."

I did write, though this greatly tired me. But I was getting better every day. In another two weeks I was able to leave my bedroom.

I introduced Clerval to the professors, but found that I could not discuss science. Since that fatal night, I could not bear to even look at a chemical instrument. Henry saw that I hated the room which had been my laboratory, and he had everything removed from my view.

Henry had come to the university to study Mideastern languages, such as Arabic and Persian. I decided to begin the same studies. I felt great relief in being a student with my friend.

Summer passed. I was going to return to Geneva at the end of autumn, but we were busy. Then winter and snow arrived. My trip was postponed until the following spring.

It was the month of May. Every day I waited for the letter from my father saying when I should come home. Henry asked if I wanted would allow me to say good-bye to Germany. I agreed to this plan with pleasure.

Two weeks passed. My health and spirits gained strength from the healthy air I breathed. Henry taught me to love nature and the cheerful faces of children again. Excellent friend! How you loved me! I became the same happy creature who a few years ago had no sorrow or care.

We returned to our college on a Sunday afternoon. Everyone we met appeared happy. My own spirits were high, and I walked along with feelings of delight.

CHAPTER SIX

The Death of William

When I returned, I found the following letter from my father:

My dear Victor,
I know you have been waiting for a letter to set the date of your return home. I was going to simply mention a date, but that would be cruel. How can I explain our tragedy? Even now your eyes are searching this page for the words that will reveal the horrible news.
William is dead! That sweet child, whose smiles warmed my heart, who was so gentle and happy! Victor, he is murdered!

FRANKENSTEIN

Last Thursday we all went for a walk near the lake. The evening was warm and peaceful. It was already dark before we thought of returning. It was then we discovered that William was missing. He had been playing hide-and-seek with Ernest. We searched for hours, but could not find him.

We went to the house, but he was not there. We returned outside with torches. About five in the morning I discovered my lovely boy stretched on the grass, pale and motionless. The print of the murderer's finger was on his neck.

He was carried home. When Elizabeth saw William's neck, she clasped her hands and cried, "O God! I have murdered my darling child!"

She fainted. When she recovered, she explained that William had begged her to let him wear a locket that night. It was gold, with a tiny portrait of your mother. This locket is gone. It must have been what the murderer was after.

Come, dearest Victor. Only you can comfort Elizabeth. Come with kindness for those who love you, and not with hatred for your enemies.

Your loving father,
Alphonse Frankenstein
Geneva, May 12th

I threw the letter on the table and covered my face with my hands. Tears gushed from Henry's eyes. "What do you intend to do?" he asked.

"I will go to Geneva. Help me order a carriage."

My journey was very sad. The road to Geneva, which ran by the side of the lake, became narrower as I approached my hometown. I wept like a child. "Dear mountains! My own beautiful lake! How do you welcome me? Your peaks are clear. The sky and lake are blue and calm. Is this to predict peace, or to mock my unhappiness?"

It was completely dark when I arrived at the town. The gates were already shut, and so I was locked out. I decided to visit the area where William had been murdered. During this short trip I saw the lightning playing on the peak of Mount Blanc. The storm rumbled, and lightning cracked through the sky.

I clasped my hands and shouted, "William, dear angel! This is your funeral song!"

As I said these words, I saw a figure move behind a clump of trees near me. I stood still and looked. It was gigantic—moving oddly. I knew what it was! The demon! What was he doing there? Could he be the murderer of my brother?

My teeth chattered and I leaned against a tree for support. The figure passed me quickly and I lost it in the gloom. I thought of chasing the devil, but it would have been useless. A flash of lightning showed that he was hanging on the rocks of Mount Salêve. He soon reached the top and disappeared.

Nearly two years had passed since that awful night when I had given life to the monster. And now he was here, alive—and my own brother dead. Could it be possible? Could this have been *his* crime? Alas! I had turned loose into the world a villain! Had he murdered my brother?

I spent the night, cold and wet, in the open air. At dawn, I went quickly to my father's house. My first thought was to tell what I knew of the murderer. But I paused when I thought about the story that I had to tell. People would think I was insane. And could he even be caught? Who could arrest a creature that could climb the sides of Mount Salêve? I decided to remain silent.

Ernest heard me arrive and came to greet me. "Welcome, Victor," he said. "Three months ago you would have found us all joyous. But now all we can share is sadness and misery!"

I tried to calm my crying brother. I asked him about my father and Elizabeth.

"Elizabeth needs the most comfort," said Ernest. "She blames herself for William's death. But since the murderer has been discovered—"

"The murderer discovered? Good God! How can that be? He was free last night!"

"What do you mean?" replied my brother. "The murderer is found! No one would believe it at first. To think that Justine Moritz murdered our brother!"

"Justine Moritz? Poor girl. Is she the accused? That can't be. No one believes it, do they, Ernest?"

"No one did at first. But several facts came out that have almost forced us to believe. And Justine has been acting oddly. I'm afraid it leaves little hope for doubt."

Ernest explained that on the day of the murder Justine fell ill. She was bedridden for several days. One of the servants discovered the locket in Justine's pocket. The servant went to a judge, and Justine was arrested.

This was a strange tale, but I had great doubts. I replied, "You are all mistaken. I know the murderer. Justine is innocent."

At that instant, my father entered. He tried to welcome me cheerfully.

Ernest exclaimed, "Papa, Victor says that he knows who murdered William!"

"We do, too," replied my father sadly.

"No, Father. Justine is innocent," I said.

"If she is, God forbid that she is found guilty. She is to be tried today. I sincerely hope that she will be cleared."

Elizabeth walked in and hugged me warmly. "Your arrival," she said, "fills me with hope. Perhaps you will find some way to clear Justine. Alas! If she is found guilty, all joy will leave me."

"She is innocent," I said. "That will be proved at the trial."

"How kind and generous you are! Everyone else believes in her guilt. To see them side against her has left me hopeless."

Elizabeth was weeping bitterly.

"Dry your tears," said my father. "If she is innocent as you believe, we must rely on the justice of our laws."

CHAPTER SEVEN

The Death of Justine

The trial was set for eleven o'clock. My father, Elizabeth, and Ernest were called as witnesses. I felt ill. If Justine *were* found guilty, it would be because of what *I had created*. I would have confessed to the murder to save Justine, but no one would have believed me. I had been in Germany at the time of the murder.

Several strange facts were presented. Justine had been out on the night of the murder. In the morning a market woman spotted her not far from where the body was found. Justine returned to the house around eight that morning. When she saw William's body, she cried and screamed.

She spent the next several days in bed. But the most serious evidence was still to come. The gold locket was brought out which the servant had found in Justine's pocket. Elizabeth took the stand and said that it was the same locket she had placed around William's neck just an hour before he had been murdered.

Justine was called to the stand to defend herself. She explained that she had spent the evening at the house of an aunt. On her return to Geneva, she met a man who asked her if she had seen William. She was alarmed to find out that he was missing. She spent several hours looking for him. Then the town gates were shut and she was forced to spend several hours in a barn. Towards morning she slept for a few minutes. She awoke when she heard some steps. She left the barn to try to find William. If she had gone near the spot where his body was found, she did not realize it. She could not explain how the gold locket ended up in her pocket.

That night I was in misery. In the morning I went to the court. The jury had cast their ballots. White for innocent. Black for guilty. They were all black! Justine was going to be hanged!

Words cannot express the despair that I suffered. And then we heard that Justine had already *confessed!* What could this mean?

We soon heard that Justine wished to see Elizabeth. We entered the gloomy prison chamber. Justine was sitting on some straw at the far end. Her hands were chained. Her head rested on her knees. She and Elizabeth both wept.

"My poor girl," said Elizabeth. "I believed you were innocent until I heard that you had confessed. If you tell me that report is false, I will believe you."

"I did confess," Justine admitted. "But I confessed a lie. Ever since I was found guilty, my priest has tortured me. He said I would suffer when I died if I did not confess. What could I do?"

"Oh, Justine!" said Elizabeth. "Forgive me for having doubted you. But do not fear. I will prove your innocence. You will not die!"

Justine shook her head sadly. "I do not fear to die," she said. "I leave a sad and bitter world."

I uttered a groan that came from deep in my soul. Justine approached me and said, "Dear sir, you are very kind to visit me. I hope you do not believe that I am guilty."

I could not answer.

"No, Justine," said Elizabeth. "He has said all along that you are innocent."

"I truly thank him. I can die in peace now that I know you and this kind gentleman believe I am innocent." She turned to Elizabeth. "Farewell, sweet lady. May heaven bless you. May this be the last tragedy that you ever suffer!"

And the next morning Justine died. She was hanged as a murderess!

Oh, how my heart was tortured! When I saw how Elizabeth suffered, I felt worse. This was all my doing! And my father's sorrow, and the gloom of our home. It was all the work of my hands!

And so William and Justine were the first victims of my unholy work.

CHAPTER EIGHT

Into the Mountains

Justine died, and I was alive. And I was the true murderer! A weight of despair pressed on my heart. Sleep fled from my eyes. I became sick again. I avoided everyone. All sounds of joy or comfort were torture to me. Solitude was my only comfort—deep, dark, death-like solitude.

The family retreated to our country house. I welcomed this change. In Geneva, the town gates were shut at ten o'clock every night, and it was impossible to remain on the lake after that hour. But now I was free to take the boat out onto the water at night to weep. I sometimes wished the waters would close over me forever.

But what about Elizabeth? I thought. *What about Father and Ernest?* I could not leave them unprotected from the monster. I would be afraid as long as anyone I loved was still alive.

I tried to clear my mind by taking long walks. One day, I rode a horse towards the nearby Alpine valleys. I wanted to forget my sorrows in the beauty of the mountains. I headed towards the valley of Chamounix. Six years had passed since I last visited. *I* was a changed wreck of a man, but the mountains still looked the same.

When the roadway became more rugged, I stabled the horse in a village and hired a mule. The weather was fine. It was about the middle of the month of August. It had been two months since the death of Justine. As I continued my journey, I began to feel much better. The mountains, the river, and the waterfalls all spoke of a power as mighty as God.

The very winds soothed my soul. But then I would find myself returning to grief again, so I would urge the mule forward. I tried desperately to forget the world, my fears, and most of all, myself. I often threw myself on the grass, weighed down by horror and despair.

Finally I arrived at the village of Chamounix. For a short time I stood at the window of the inn. I watched the pale lightning that played above Mount Blanc. I listened to the rushing of the river. Then I placed my head upon my pillow and sleep crept over me.

The next morning when I awoke, the rain was pouring down. Thick mists hid the peaks of the mountains. My mule was brought to the door. I decided to climb to the snowy, icy top of Montanvert. The majesty of nature had always helped me to forget the cares of life.

The path was steep. It was nearly noon when I arrived at the top of the rise. I walked down onto a huge glacier of ice. The surface was uneven, like the waves of a sea, and it took nearly two hours to cross it. Above the glacier rose Mount Blanc. I sat to enjoy this shining sea of ice winding among the mountains. My heart swelled with joy.

Suddenly, I saw the figure of a man moving towards me with superhuman speed. He leaped over the cracks in the ice. As the shape came nearer, I saw that it was the monster whom I had created! I trembled with rage and horror. I decided to fight with him to the death!

Then, there he was! His face showed pain and hatred. It was almost too horrible for human eyes.

"Devil!" I exclaimed. "How dare you approach me! Be gone, disgusting insect! Or stay so that I may trample you to dust! If only your death could bring back those whom you have murdered!"

"I expected you to act this way," said the demon. "But if you agree to what I ask, I will leave you at peace. If you refuse, I will fill the jaws of death with the blood of all your friends."

"Disgusting monster! Come on, then, so I may end the life which I so carelessly started."

My rage was without end. I sprang on him.

He easily escaped me and said, "Be calm! I beg you to hear me before you strike. Life is dear to me, and I will defend it. Remember, you have made me more powerful than yourself. Oh, Frankenstein, do not be fair to everyone but me. Remember that I am your creature. I was born with a good heart. Misery made me a monster. Make me happy, and I will again be good."

"Be gone! I will not hear you. There can be no understanding between you and me. We are enemies. Be gone, or let us test our strength in a fight, in which one must fall."

"Why do you refuse to listen and understand me? Believe me, Frankenstein, I was gentle. My soul glowed with love and kindness. But if *you* hate me, what hope can I have for your fellow men? You owe me something for creating me. But they owe me nothing. If mankind knew about me, they would destroy me. They would hate me. So why shouldn't I hate *them*? I will make no peace with my enemies. I am miserable, and they shall share my misery.

"Yet it is in your power to help me," he went on. "Listen to my tale. *Hear* me. Then, if you are still able to, destroy the work of your hands."

"Why do you force me to think about these things?" I replied. "I shudder to remember what I've done. Be gone!"

"I demand that you listen to me," he said. "Hear my tale. It is long and strange, and this place is too cold and wet for you. Come to my hut upon the mountain. Before night falls, you will have heard my story. Then the decision rests on you. I will either leave the world of man forever, or I will become the curse of your fellow creatures and the cause of your own destruction."

As he said this, he led the way across the ice. I thought of his words and decided to follow. I had been his creator. I should at least listen to his tale. Was he the murderer of my brother? His story would reveal if that were true. I owed something to him as his creator. I ought to try to make him happy before I complained of his wickedness.

We crossed the ice and climbed a rock. The air was cold, and it began to rain again. We entered the hut. He seemed happy to be there. My own heart was heavy and depressed. But I agreed to listen. I sat myself by the fire, and my awful companion began his tale.

CHAPTER NINE

The Monster Begins His Tale

It is hard to remember my first days after I came into being. It was a confusing time. Everything happened at once. I saw, felt, heard, and smelled at the same time. I wandered about outside between buildings, not knowing what to do. The light bothered my eyes. The heat tired me as I walked.

Finally, I found my way to a shady area. This was the forest outside the town. Here I rested beside a brook. I ate some berries which I found hanging on the trees or lying on the ground. I quenched my thirst at the brook. Then, lying down, I was overcome by sleep.

It was dark when I awoke. I was cold and frightened. Before I left your apartment I had covered myself with some clothes, but these could not protect me from the damp night. I was a poor, helpless, miserable creature who under-stood nothing. Pain surrounded me on all sides.

I sat down and wept.

Several changes of day and night passed before I was able to understand all my senses. One day I found a fire left by some travelers. I was delighted by its warmth. In my joy I thrust my hand into the live embers, but quickly drew it out again with a cry of pain.

I studied this fire. I quickly gathered branches to add to it. I soon found that the fire gave light as well as heat. I found some roasted food in the fire that the travelers had left. I tried to place my own food on the fire. The berries were spoiled by this, but the nuts and roots tasted better.

Food became scarce. I often spent the whole day searching for a few acorns. I decided to leave the woods. After three days I came to the open country. It had snowed, and my feet hurt with cold as a walked over the great fields of this thick, icy whiteness.

I came upon a small hut, and went in to find warmth. There a man sat by a fire. When he turned and saw me, he screamed and fled! This surprised me. I found his breakfast and ate most of it. The rest I took with me.

I walked still more, and finally I arrived at a village. I looked through the windows at the

tables of food and the warm fires. How wonderful it seemed! I entered one of the cottages. But I had hardly stepped inside before the children shrieked and one woman fainted. The whole village was awakened. Some people fled and some attacked me. I was terribly bruised by stones. I ran back to the open country!

I quickly took shelter in a wooden hut built against the back of a cottage. On one side was a pigsty, and on the other, a pool of water. The floor was raised and perfectly dry. The hut was close to the stone chimney of the cottage, so it was warm. I spread some clean straw and lay down to rest.

Suddenly I heard a noise outside. Looking through a small crack, I saw a young woman walking with a pail on her head. She was neat but poorly dressed. Her face looked gentle and sad. Not much later the girl returned with the pail partly filled with milk. A sad young man met her. He carried her pail to the cottage.

I examined my hut. On the cottage-side wall there was a boarded-up window. Between the boards, I looked through and saw a room. It was clean, but with little furniture. An old man sat near a fire. He took up something made of wood and began to make sounds sweeter than the voices of the birds. The girl sat near him. It was a lovely sight, even to a poor creature like me, who had never seen anything beautiful before. The old man played a song that brought tears to the eyes of the girl. He looked at her and smiled with incredible kindness.

I felt a strange mixture of pain and pleasure. I looked away, unable to stand these emotions.

The young man returned with a load of wood, and the girl added some to the fire. Next, the young man left to dig in the garden. After a while, the girl came to help him carry some things into the cottage.

Later, the family sat down to eat their small meal. Night quickly set in. To my extreme wonder, I found that the cottagers could make light with candles. The old man again made some music. Then the young man began. He did not play, but he spoke sounds. I now know that he read aloud, but at that time I knew nothing of words or letters. Finally, the family put out their lights and went to sleep.

I could not sleep. I thought of the events of the day. What struck me most were the gentle manners of these people. I longed to join them, but dared not. I remembered too well the treatment I had suffered the night before from the cruel villagers. I decided that I would remain quietly in my hut, watching the cottagers.

CHAPTER TEN

Learning Language

The next days passed in the same way as the ones before. The young man was busy out-of-doors. The girl worked inside the house. The old man, whom I soon understood to be blind, spent the hours playing music or thinking.

They were not completely happy. The young man and the girl often wept. I saw no cause for their unhappiness, but I was deeply touched by it. If such lovely creatures were miserable, then it was not strange that I was sad. Yet why were they unhappy? It seemed to me that they had a delightful house and everything they could want. Did their tears really express pain?

Finally, after some time of watching them, I figured out that the family was very poor. This was part of the reason they were so sad. They had very little to eat—just vegetables from the garden and milk from one cow. The two younger cottagers often gave food to the old man while they took none for themselves. This kindness touched me deeply. Each night I had been stealing a part of their food for myself. But when I found that this caused them pain, I stopped. I satisfied myself with berries, nuts, and roots. I also helped the cottagers by collecting wood for them at night. They were surprised by these gifts, but I did not reveal myself to them.

I also learned that they used sounds to tell each other things. These words they spoke could bring smiles or sadness. I wanted to learn how to talk like this. After many months, I learned the names of several objects. I learned the words "fire," "milk," "bread," and "wood." I also learned the names of the cottagers themselves. The girl was "sister" or "Agatha," and the young man was "Felix," "brother," or "son." The old man was "father." I learned but did not understand words like "good," "dearest," and "unhappy."

There was little to do in the frosty season. Felix read to the old man and Agatha. This reading had puzzled me at first. But over time I discovered that he spoke many of the same sounds when he read as when he talked. I longed to understand these written words, too. I knew I could not meet the cottagers until I could speak and understand their language.

I admired the beauty and grace of my cottagers. But how terrified I was when I viewed *myself* in a pool of water! At first I jumped back, unable to believe that it was I in the mirror. I was filled with bitter feelings of gloom and shame.

As the sun became warmer and the light of day longer, the snow vanished. I saw the bare trees and the black earth. Felix was busier now. Several new kinds of plants sprang up in the garden, and they had more food to eat.

My life in my hut was unchanging. At night I went into the woods to collect food. I brought back firewood for the cottage. I also cleared their path of any snow. These things greatly pleased and surprised them. Once or twice I heard them use the words "good spirit" and "wonderful." But I did not then understand these words.

More and more I wanted to understand why Felix and Agatha were so sad. Their blind, gentle father could not always cheer them. I wanted to find a way to make them happier. I knew I could not appear before them, but I worked harder than ever on my speech.

The pleasant showers and warmth of spring greatly changed the earth. The birds sang in more cheerful notes. The leaves began to bud on the trees. Happy, happy earth! My spirits were lifted by the loveliness of nature. The past was wiped from my memory. The present was peaceful. And the future seemed full of hope and joy.

I now come to an important part of my story. These events changed me. They changed from what I had been to what I am now.

One beautiful spring day, the cottagers were resting from their work. The father was playing his guitar, but Felix was gloomy, often sighing. His father asked what had caused this sorrow. Felix answered in a cheerful tone, and the old man had turned back to his music—when someone tapped at the door.

It was a lady on horseback. She was dressed in a dark suit and covered with a thick black veil.

The stranger spoke the name of Felix in a sweet accent. Her voice was unlike those of my friends. Felix came up to her quickly. She lifted her veil. Her hair was shining black. Her eyes were dark but gentle, and her skin was beautifully fair.

Felix seemed enchanted when he saw her. Every hint of sorrow vanished from his face. She wiped a few tears from her lovely eyes. Felix kissed her hand and called her "Safie." She smiled. He helped her off the horse and led her into the cottage.

The stranger had a language of her own. The cottagers made many signs which I did not understand. I began to realize that the stranger was trying to learn their language. I decided that I should make use of her lessons. The stranger learned about twenty words in one short lesson. Most of them were words I already knew.

Joy now took the place of sadness on the faces of my friends. Safie's smiles brightened the cottage. She had come to stay, it seemed. As she learned the language of the cottagers, I listened and learned also. Safie and I both improved quickly. In two months, I began to understand most of the words spoken by the cottagers.

I also learned how to write letters, as Felix and Agatha taught Safie to write. This opened a wide field of wonder to me. I learned of many things that affect men—great wealth, terrible poverty, class, and noble blood. I learned that human beings valued their name and where they came from. And what was I? I knew nothing about my creation or my creator. I had no money, no friends. I was hideously deformed and disgusting to look at. When I looked around I saw and heard of no one like me. Was I a monster?

I also learned about men and women. I learned about the birth and growth of children. I heard of mother, father, brother, sister. I learned about all the relationships which bind human beings to each other. But where were *my* friends and relatives? I had always been the same size. I had never seen a being who looked like me. What was I? I could only answer my own questions with groans. Miserable, unhappy monster!

CHAPTER ELEVEN

The Hour of Trial

Some time passed before I learned the history of my friends. The name of the old man was DeLacey. He was from a good family in France. He had been a wealthy man, well respected and loved. He and his family had lived in a city called Paris, surrounded by friends.

Safie's father was the reason they were now poor. He was a Muslim Turkish merchant who had lived in Paris for many years. For some reason he was seized and thrown into prison, tried and sentenced to death. All of Paris was furious. It was believed that his religion and wealth had been the actual reasons for his arrest.

Felix had been present at the trial. He was angry when he heard the decision of the court. He made a solemn vow to help the Turk escape from prison. The man promised Safie's hand in marriage to Felix. They would be married as soon as the man was moved to a safe place.

With Felix's help, Safie's father escaped from prison the day before he was to be executed. They fled to Italy, and the man waited for his chance to escape to Turkey.

Felix and Safie spoke different languages, but somehow they fell in love. They were happily planning their marriage when shocking news arrived from Paris.

DeLacey and Agatha had been thrown into prison for Felix's crime. When Felix explained that he had to return to France, the Turk promised that Safie would wait for Felix.

But Felix was sent to prison as well. The family remained behind bars for five months before the trial took place. Their fortune was taken away and they were forced to leave France forever. They made their way to Germany and found a cottage to rent. Here they managed to live with little money and little food.

When the Turk learned that the family was poor, he refused to let his daughter marry Felix. He was going to force her to return with him to Turkey, but Safie learned the name of the spot where Felix was living. She took some jewels and some money and departed for Germany. And now that she had found Felix, she planned to stay.

Such was the history of my beloved cottagers.

And now I must tell you about something that happened in August that changed my happy life.

One night, while gathering wood and food in the forest, I found a leather suitcase filled with clothes and books. I eagerly returned with it to my hut. The books were written in the language I was learning from the cottagers. Slowly I started sounding out the words and reading them. One was a history book. Another was about great thoughts and ideas. One was called *Paradise Lost*, about God's creation of Adam.

These books gave me new feelings and things to think about. I felt joy—and great sorrow. I could relate to Adam and other heroes. And yet, I knew I was not really like other humans. How could I be? I was hideous. I was gigantic. Who was I? *What* was I? Where did I come from?

Then I read something that made me question my life even more. When I first arrived in the hut, I had discovered a book in the pocket of the coat I had taken from your laboratory. Now I began to study it. It was your journal of my creation. Surely you remember it. Here it is. You wrote that you thought I was horrible and disgusting. I grew sick as I read. "Hateful day when I received life!" I exclaimed. "Evil creator! Why did you form a monster so hideous that even *you* turned from me in disgust?" God had created man to be so beautiful—like the cottagers. But my own creator had created me to be a monster.

I became more depressed and lonely as I read these things. I decided that my only hope for happiness was to show myself to the cottagers and win their friendship. Would they turn away someone who asked for friendship?

I would wait a few months and learn more language. This way I would be able to speak with confidence. But I would enter the cottage when the blind old man was alone. The sight of me disgusted people, but my voice was not terrible. If I could gain the friendship of old DeLacey, then the younger cottagers would accept me.

Autumn came and went. A year had now passed since I awoke into life. One day Safie, Agatha, and Felix took a long country walk. The old man was alone. All was silent in and around the cottage. This was the hour of trial. My heart beat quickly as I approached the door of the cottage and knocked.

"Who is there?" said the old man. "Come in."

I entered. "Pardon this interruption," I said. "I am a traveler who needs a little rest. Might I rest a few minutes before your fire?"

"Enter," said DeLacey. "I am blind, so I am afraid I will find it difficult to serve food to you. Unfortunately my children are away from home."

"Do not trouble yourself, my kind host. I have food. It is only warmth and rest that I need."

I sat down, and a silence followed. Then the old man spoke. "By your language I suppose you are my countryman. Are you French?"

"No. But I was educated by a French family. I am seeking the protection of some friends—secret friends—whom I truly love."

"Are they Germans?"

"No, they are French. But let us change the subject. I am an unfortunate, lonely creature.

I have no relative or friend upon earth. These kind people—my secret friends—have never seen me and know little of me. I am full of fears. If I fail to gain their friendship, I will be an outcast in the world forever."

"The hearts of men are full of brotherly love. If these friends are good and kind, do not despair," said the old man.

"They *are* kind. They are the most excellent creatures in the world, but they may not love me. I am harmless. And I have been good to them. But where they should see a kind friend, they may only see… a monster."

"That is indeed unfortunate. Can you change their minds?"

"I am about to try. That is why I feel so nervous and afraid. I love these friends, but they may think I wish to injure them."

"Where do these friends live?"

"Near this spot."

"Perhaps I may be able to help you," said the old man. "I am blind and cannot judge you by your face, but there is something in your words which tells me that you are honest. It will give me true pleasure to help you."

"Excellent man! How can I thank you?" I cried. "You are the first person who has spoken kindly to me. I shall be forever grateful."

"May I know the names of your friends?"

At that moment I heard the steps of the young cottagers. I had not a moment to lose. I seized the hand of the old man and cried, "Save and protect me! You and your family are the friends whom I seek. Do not desert me in the hour of trial!"

"Great God!" exclaimed the frightened old man. "Who are you?"

Just then the cottage door was opened. Felix, Safie, and Agatha entered. Who can describe their horror upon seeing me? Agatha fainted. Safie rushed out of the cottage. Felix pushed me to the ground and struck me violently with a stick. I could have torn him limb from limb, but my heart sank within me and I stopped myself. I ran from the cottage and escaped into the woods.

Cursed, cursed creator! Why did I live? I know not. I should have felt despair, but my first feelings were of rage and revenge. I could have destroyed the cottage. I would have enjoyed the shrieks and misery of the cottagers.

What a miserable night I passed! I sank on the damp grass in the sickness of despair. There was no one who would pity or help me. Should I feel kindness towards my enemies? No. From that moment, I declared everlasting war against the species of man, and especially against the man who had created me—Victor Frankenstein!

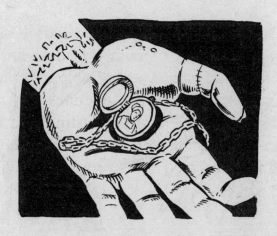

CHAPTER TWELVE

Revenge!

I slept. When I woke it was already night. I returned to the cottage. I crept into my hut and waited for the family to arise. The sun rose high in the heavens, but the cottagers did not appear.

Finally Felix arrived with another man. "Do you understand," said the man, "that if you leave, you must still pay three months' rent? Please take some days to think this over."

"It is useless," replied Felix. "We cannot live here. My father is in great danger. My wife and my sister will never recover from their horror."

Felix and the man left. I never saw any of the family again.

I spent the rest of the day in my hut. Feelings of revenge and hatred filled my heart. That night I lit a tree branch and danced around the cottage with fury. The moon sank. With a loud scream I lit the straw. The cottage was quickly surrounded by the flames. I left the scene and sought shelter in the woods.

And now, with the world before me, where was I to go? The thought of *you* crossed my mind. You were my father. Who else could I turn to? You had written in your journal that Geneva, Switzerland, was your hometown. I decided to seek you out. But how?

I knew I must travel to the southwest, and the sun was my only guide. I could ask no one for directions, but had signs to follow. I traveled only at night, trudging on through rain and snow. I managed to find a map which helped me. The nearer I got to Switzerland, the more I felt revenge in my heart. I never rested. Over snow and ice, I kept on.

The earth began to look green again when I reached the border of Switzerland. And then something happened which increased my feelings of horror and anger.

One morning, I was walking beside a deep and rapid river. I heard voices and quickly hid from view. A young girl came running towards the spot where I was hidden. Suddenly her foot slipped and she fell into the rapid stream.

I jumped in and saved her, dragging her to shore. She was unconscious, and I tried to wake her. I was interrupted by the approach of a man. He tore the girl from my arms and ran towards the wood. But then he turned, aimed a gun at me, and fired! I sank to the ground in pain.

This was my reward! I had saved a human being, and in return I received a wound which shattered the flesh and bone. I vowed eternal hatred and revenge against all mankind.

For some weeks, I led a miserable life in the woods as I tried to cure my wound. The pain was terrible—from the wound and the injustice. When my wound healed, I continued my journey. Two months later I reached Geneva.

It was evening when I arrived. I hid among the fields that surround the town. I was just falling off to sleep when a beautiful child came running through the field. As I watched him, an idea came to me. This little boy was too young to be afraid of ugliness. If I could befriend a young person, I would not be so alone on this earth.

I seized the young boy as he passed. But as soon as he saw me, he placed his hands over his eyes and screamed!

I drew his hand from his face and said, "Child, I won't hurt you. Listen to me."

He struggled and cried, "Let me go! Monster! You'll eat me and tear me to pieces! Let me go, or I will tell my papa!"

"Boy, you will never see your father again. You must come with me," I explained.

"Let me go! My papa is Mr. Frankenstein. He will punish you! You better *not* keep me!"

"Frankenstein?" I said. "You belong to my enemy! You will be my first victim."

The child struggled and called me names. My heart broke. I tried to silence him—and in a moment he lay limp at my feet, dead.

I had felt revenge! Clapping my hands, I exclaimed, "I too can create misery! The death of this child will bring despair to Frankenstein. And a thousand other miseries will torment and destroy him."

I saw something glittering on the child's shirt. It was a portrait of a lovely woman. For a few moments I gazed at it with delight. But then my rage returned. I would never know the love of a beautiful woman. She would have been disgusted and frightened by me.

Seeking a hiding place, I entered a barn. There I found a woman sleeping on some straw. I bent over her and whispered, "Awake, fair lady. I would give my life to have one look of affection from your eyes."

The sleeper stirred. A thrill of terror ran through me. Would she indeed awake, and see me, and curse me? If she saw me, she would know the face of the murderer! In a moment of madness, I placed the locket with the portrait in one of the folds of her dress. Now everyone would suspect this woman as the murderer and would never seek me! She moved again, and I fled.

For some days, I haunted the spot where these scenes had taken place. Finally I wandered towards these mountains.

I am alone and miserable. I have only one hope of ever being loved. A woman as deformed as myself would love me.

This being you must create!

CHAPTER THIRTEEN

The Awful Promise

The monster finished speaking. He waited for me to reply, but I did not understand what he wanted from me.

He continued, "You must create a female for me. You are the only one who can do this. I demand it of you."

My anger had melted as he told of his peaceful life. But then he had described how he murdered William and Justine. Rage burned within me.

"I *do* refuse it," I replied. "You wish me to create another being like yourself? Together you might destroy the world! Be gone! You can torture me, but I will never agree."

"Don't you even care?" replied the monster. "If I cannot know love, I will cause fear. I will hate you forever. I will work at your destruction. I will not finish until I destroy your heart. You will curse the hour of your own birth."

An inhuman rage filled his face. It was almost too horrible to look at. But then he calmed himself again.

"I demand a female creature who is as hideous as myself," he went on. "If you agree, no one shall ever see us again. We will go to the vast wild regions of South America. We will make a hut and sleep on dried leaves. The sun will shine on us and will ripen our food. We will be peaceful."

"You say you will leave the places of man," I replied. "But you will still want the kindness of humans. You will return, and you will again meet with their hatred. And then you will have a companion to help you with their destruction! This cannot be. Do not argue. I cannot agree."

"I swear to you that we will stay away from man. My feelings of despair will be gone, because I will have someone who understands me. My life will flow quietly away. In my dying moments I will not curse my maker."

His words had a strange effect on me. I pitied him and wanted to comfort him. But when I looked at him, my heart sickened and my feelings were those of horror and hatred.

"You swear," I said, "to be harmless. But you have already shown your wicked side. Perhaps even *this* is a trick!"

"I must not be fooled with! I demand an answer!" the monster roared.

I thought for a long time. Finally I agreed to do as he wished. "I will deliver a female into your hands," I said, "but I must have your solemn promise that you will leave Europe. You must stay away from man forever."

"I swear," he cried, "by the sun, and by the blue sky of heaven, and by the fire of love that burns in my heart. If you grant my prayer, you will never see me again. Depart to your home and begin your work. I will eagerly be watching its progress. When you are ready I shall appear."

Saying this, he suddenly left me. Perhaps he was fearful that I would change my mind. I saw him descend the mountain with greater speed than the flight of an eagle. I quickly lost sight of him among the waves of the sea of ice.

Night had long since come by the time I reached a resting place halfway down the mountain. The stars shone through the clouds. The dark pine trees rose before me. Here and there a broken tree lay on the ground. I wept bitterly. Clasping my hands, I exclaimed, "Oh! Stars and clouds and winds, are you here to mock me? If you pity me, end my feelings—and take my memory. Let me become nothing. Or depart and leave me in darkness."

These were my wild thoughts as the eternal twinkling of the stars weighed upon me. I listened to the wind, hoping that every blast would take me away.

It was morning before I arrived at the village of Chamounix. I returned immediately to Geneva. My family was alarmed by how starved and wild I looked, but I answered no questions.

CHAPTER FOURTEEN

To England

Weeks passed. I did not have the courage to again take up my work. I feared the anger of the monster, but I was overcome with disgust at creating another creature.

To create a female, I would need to spend several months in study. There was a doctor in England who did research on female anatomy. I thought of asking my father's permission to visit England, but every day I thought of a new excuse not to go.

I knew my father would not understand. My health was much improved and my spirits were better. He would wonder why I'd want to leave.

One day, my father remarked on my recovery.

"I am happy to see that you seem to be returning to yourself," he said. "But you still avoid our company. Yesterday an idea came to me. I know that you love Elizabeth…"

"My dear father, I love Elizabeth dearly."

"Then tell me… Is it not time you two marry?"

Alas! The idea was horrible to me. I could not marry Elizabeth with the creature's deadly threat hanging around my neck. I had to do my duty first. I had to go to England. I refused to perform my disgusting work in my father's house. I had to remove myself from all I loved.

I explained to my father that I wished to visit England—for no more than a year. Of course I did not tell him why I wanted to go. My father agreed to the trip. He and Elizabeth arranged to have Henry join me. I pledged my love to Elizabeth and agreed to marry when I returned.

At the end of September, I left Switzerland with all my chemicals and instruments. I was miserable during the trip. But Henry? He was alive to every new scene. He pointed out to me the shifting colors of the landscape. He spoke of the clouds and beauty of the sky.

Ah, Henry! My beloved friend! He was formed in the "very poetry of nature." His soul overflowed with affection. His friendship was wonderful. And where is he now? Is this lovely being lost forever? No, it is not so. His body has decayed, but his spirit still comforts me.

Pardon this gush of sorrow, Captain Walton. These words are useless, I know. But they soothe my heart. I will continue with my tale. . . .

I first saw the white cliffs of England on a clear morning at the end of December. We spent several months in the wonderful city of London. Normally this journey would have given me great pleasure. But a curse had come over me. I visited people only for the information they could give me. Company was annoying to me. I had gruesome work to do—collecting parts once again under cover of night, and packing them away out of sight of Henry.

Several months later, we received a letter from a friend in Scotland. He mentioned the beauties of his country and asked us to visit him in Perth. We decided to leave for Scotland in March. I packed up my equipment and the materials I had collected. I would finish my work there.

We toured all through northern England and arrived in Perth at the end of July. I had now ignored my promise to the monster for some time. He would be angry, I knew. Was he still in Switzerland? Were my relatives in danger? Or was the monster following me, as he said he would? I feared for Henry's life more than my own.

I told Henry that I wished to make a tour of Scotland alone. I crossed the northern highlands and settled on one of the remote Orkney Islands. It was hardly more than a rock.

Only five people lived on the island, and there were only three huts. I rented the empty hut, which had two rooms. The roof had fallen in, the walls were not plastered, and the door was off its hinges. I ordered it to be repaired, bought some furniture, and moved my equipment in.

I spent my mornings working. In the evenings I walked on the stony beach. Every day my work became more horrible. Sometimes I could not force myself to enter my laboratory. At other times I worked day and night. Before, I had been blind to the horror of my work. I had been too excited to realize what I was doing. But now my heart was sickened at the work of my hands.

As I worked, I feared that the monster was there—watching me. I often kept my eyes on the ground as I walked the beach in case I should have to see that horrible face.

But I worked on and on. All the parts I had gathered in England were becoming another creature under my hands—a creature who would receive life from me.

CHAPTER FIFTEEN

A Promise Broken

One night I was sitting in my laboratory. The moon was just rising from the sea. I was trying to decide whether or not I should continue my work. I became lost in thought.

Three years before, I had created a monster who had done evil. This filled my heart with the most painful regret. I was now about to create *another* being. What if she became ten thousand times more vicious than the monster? *He* had sworn to stay away from mankind, but *she* had not. What if she refused to agree to a promise made before her creation? They might even hate each other.

And—horrors—what if they wanted children? A race of devils might be created! Did I have the right to curse future generations this way?

I trembled and came out of my deep thoughts. Looking up, I saw the monster at the window! A ghastly grin wrinkled his lips as he gazed on me. Yes, he had followed me in my travels!

As I looked at him, his face seemed filled with evil. I went mad with the idea that I had promised to create another like him. Trembling with passion, I tore to pieces the "thing" which I had been working on. The monster saw me destroy the female creature, and he sent up a howl of despair—and revenge.

I heard heavy footsteps along the passage. The door opened and the creature appeared. He approached me and said, "Do you dare to break your promise? Do you dare destroy my hopes?"

"Be gone! I *do* break my promise. Never will I create another like yourself."

"Slave! You are my creator, but I am your master. Obey!"

"Your threats cannot make me do wickedness. Be gone! I am firm, and your words will only increase my rage," I vowed.

The monster gnashed his teeth in anger. "Why must everyone but me have a companion? Must I be alone?" he cried. "You may hate me, but beware! I may die, but before I do—beware! For I am fearless and therefore powerful."

"Devil, cease. Do not poison the air with these sounds. I have declared my decision to you. I am no coward. Leave me. I will not yield."

"I will go. But remember: *I will be with you on your wedding night.*"

"Villain! Before you sign my death warrant, be sure that you are yourself safe!"

I would have seized him, but he escaped. In a few moments I saw him in his boat. It shot swiftly across the waters and was lost amidst the waves.

His words rang in my ears: "*I will be with you on your wedding night.*" The idea of my death did not frighten me. But when I thought of Elizabeth, tears streamed from my eyes. I would not fall without a bitter struggle.

The next morning, I unlocked the door of my laboratory. The remains of the creature were scattered on the floor. I put them in a basket with a large quantity of stones. I decided to throw them into the sea that very night.

Between two and three in the morning the moon rose. I rowed out about four miles from the shore. When the moon became covered by a thick cloud, I threw my basket into the sea. I listened to the gurgling sound as it sank. Then I rowed away from the spot.

I stretched myself out on the bottom of the boat. Clouds hid the moon. Everything was dark. In a short time I slept soundly.

When I awoke, I found that the sun had already risen. I was far from the coast and had no compass. I could sail into the wide Atlantic—or be swallowed up in the waters that roared around me. The sea was to be my grave.

"Devil, your work is already done!" I called out. At that point, I did not care about my own life. But then I thought of Elizabeth, of my father, of Ernest, and of Henry. They were all left behind! The monster might satisfy his blood-thirsty revenge by killing them!

Some hours had passed when I suddenly saw a line of land towards the south. I made a sail with part of my clothing. As I neared the land, I saw a small, neat town and a good harbor. My heart leapt with joy.

Several people crowded towards the spot where I landed. They whispered together.

"My good friends," I said in English, "will you be so kind as to tell me the name of this town?"

"You will know that soon enough," replied a man with a hoarse voice. "But methinks you won't like this place, for we hate villains here!"

I was very surprised by his rude answer. The growing crowd followed and surrounded me. An ill-looking man tapped me on the shoulder.

"Come, sir," he said. "You must follow me to Mr. Kirwin's to answer some questions."

"Who is Mr. Kirwin? What questions do I have to answer? Is not this a free country?"

"Aye, sir, free enough for honest folks. Mr. Kirwin is a judge. You are to answer questions about a gentleman who was found murdered here last night."

This answer startled me, but I soon recovered myself. I was innocent. It could easily be proved. But then I did not expect the tragedy that was about to overwhelm me.

Accused of Murder

Mr. Kirwin was a kind old man with mild manners, but he looked at me rather grimly. He called for the witnesses.

A man testified that he had been out fishing the night before with his son and brother-in-law. They returned about ten o'clock, and the witness had walked on first, carrying the fishing tackle. He struck his foot against something and fell to the ground. He had tripped on the body of a man. They carried the body to a nearby cottage and tried to revive the man, but it was no use. He appeared to be a handsome young man, about twenty five years old. He had been strangled.

My limbs trembled. It must have been the work of the monster! A mist came over my eyes. I was forced to lean on a chair for support.

Other witnesses offered more evidence. A boat with one man in it had been spotted near the crime scene. They believed it was the same boat I had just landed in.

These events were very strange. The evidence did seem to point to me, but I was confident that I would not be arrested.

Mr. Kirwin wanted to see what effect the sight of the body would have on me. I entered the room where the body lay and was led up to the coffin. There I saw the lifeless form of Henry Clerval! I gasped for breath and threw myself on the body.

"My dearest Henry! Has the work of my hands killed you as well? I have already destroyed two. But you, Henry! My friend—"

I collapsed, and I was carried out of the room.

I suffered from a terrible fever. For two months I was on the brink of death. I shouted and wailed in my fever, calling myself the murderer of William, of Justine, and of Henry. Sometimes I begged people to help me destroy the monster.

Other times I felt the fingers of the monster around my neck and I screamed. Fortunately, only Mr. Kirwin understood French. But my cries were enough to frighten the others.

After two months, I awoke to find myself in a prison, lying on a miserable bed. It was morning. When I looked around and saw the barred windows and the filth of the room, I groaned bitterly. I could not think about everything that had passed. My whole life seemed like a dream.

I soon learned that Mr. Kirwin had been very kind to me. He had put me in the best room in the prison and provided a doctor and a nurse for me. One day during my recovery, Mr. Kirwin entered. He drew up a chair and spoke to me in French.

"Immediately after you fell ill, I had all of your papers brought to me," he said. "I wanted to write to your relatives. I found several letters, including one from your father—and I wrote to him. It has been nearly two months since that time. Ah, but you are ill. You should not be disturbed at all."

"This suspense is a thousand times worse than the most horrible event. Tell me what new scene of death has occurred. Tell me whose murder I am now to mourn!" I cried.

"Your family is perfectly well," said the judge gently. "A friend has come to visit you."

He left the room, and in a moment my father entered. I stretched out my hand to him and cried, "Are you safe—and Elizabeth—and Ernest?"

My father assured me that everyone was well. He tried to be cheerful for me, but the prison was too dreary. "What a place this is, my son!" he said. "And poor Henry—"

The name of my murdered friend was a pain too great for me to handle. I shed tears. "Alas! Yes, my father," I sobbed. "Something awful hangs over me. I should have died along with Henry. Why am I, alone, meant to live?"

We were not allowed to talk for very long, but even that short visit from my father was like a visit from my good angel. Little by little, I managed to recover my health.

A month later, the season of the court sessions arrived. I had to travel nearly a hundred miles to the country town where the court was held. The grand jury rejected the case. It was proved that I was on the Orkney Islands at the time of the murder. Two weeks after my trial I was released from prison.

My father was thrilled that I was allowed to return to Switzerland. But I was not happy. All around me I saw nothing but a frightful darkness. No light broke through this gloom but the glimmer of two eyes that glared at me. Sometimes they were the eyes of Henry. Sometimes they were the watery, clouded eyes of the monster.

I had to return to Geneva to watch over my loved ones. I would wait for the murderer. I would put an end to him. We took our passage and sailed away from the Scottish shores.

CHAPTER SEVENTEEN

Home to Elizabeth

We traveled to Paris. A few days later, I received the following letter from Elizabeth:

My dear Victor,

I was thrilled to receive a letter from your father dated at Paris. I hope to see you in less than two weeks. My poor friend, how you have suffered!

Victor, you know that your parents have wished us to marry since we were young children. We were loving playmates during childhood. Now we are dear friends. But perhaps you think of me as a sister? I beg you to answer me, for you have not written me. Do you love another?

I confess that I love you. I wish to share my future with you. But I swear to you that our marriage would make me forever miserable unless it is your own free choice.

Do not let this letter disturb you. Do not answer tomorrow, or the next day, or even until you come, if it will give you pain. Your father will send me news of your health. And if I see but one smile on your lips when we meet, I shall need no other happiness.

Elizabeth Lavenza

Geneva, May 18th

Sweet Elizabeth! I would die to make her happy. I decided that the monster's threats would not delay our marriage a moment longer.

"Chase away your fears," I wrote to her. "I devote my life to you. But I have one secret, Elizabeth. It is a dreadful one. It will chill you with horror. I will share this secret with you the day after our marriage. Until then, I beg you, do not mention this."

About a week later, we returned to Geneva. Elizabeth welcomed me with warm affection. We set our wedding date for ten days later.

Dear Heavens! If I had known then what I know now—what the monster's awful plans were... But I was blind with love.

Through my father's efforts, a part of Elizabeth's inheritance had been returned to her. She now owned a small home on the shores of Lake Como. Immediately after our marriage we would go there. We would spend our first days of happiness beside the beautiful lake.

In the meantime I carried pistols and a dagger with me everywhere. I was ever on the watch for the monster and his trickery.

After our beautiful wedding, a large party gathered at my father's house. Elizabeth and I began our journey on that fair day. Those were the last moments of my life that I was happy.

On the boat, I took Elizabeth's hand. "You are so quiet, my love. Ah! I know that you have worried about me. All I want now is to enjoy the quiet of this day with you."

"Be happy, dear Victor," replied Elizabeth. "My heart is content. The scenery is beautiful. Look how the clouds embrace Mont Blanc. Look at the fish swimming in the clear lake. What a divine day! How happy and peaceful all nature is!"

The wind became a light breeze. The sun sank beneath the horizon. As we landed I felt the return of those fears which soon would cling to me forever.

CHAPTER EIGHTEEN

My Wedding Night

It was eight o'clock when we landed. We walked for a short time on the shore and then went to the inn. The wind now rose with great violence and a heavy storm blew in.

As soon as night approached, a thousand fears arose in my mind. My right hand grasped a pistol that was hidden in my coat. Every sound terrified me. But I was determined not to run away from my fears. It would not end until my life or the monster's life was ended.

Elizabeth was worried by the look on my face. She asked, "What is it that troubles you, my dear Victor? What is it you fear?"

"Oh! Peace, peace, my love," I replied. "All will be safe after this night. But this night is dreadful, very dreadful."

I passed an hour fretting and waiting. What would I do if the creature showed up? Elizabeth would be terrified! I begged her to go to our room. I would not join her until I discovered what the monster was up to.

After she left, I wandered the hallways of the inn, but there was no sign of him. Suddenly, I heard a dreadful scream. It came from our room! My arms dropped and every muscle froze. I heard another scream, and I rushed into the room!

Great God! Why did I not die right then? There was my beloved Elizabeth across the bed! Her head was hanging down. Her face was pale. Even now, I can still see it—her body flung by the monster murderer on our bridal bed.

Ah, my love, my wife—so young, so dear, so worthy! I embraced her, but her limbs were deadly still and cold. What I held in my arms was no longer the Elizabeth whom I had loved and cherished. The mark of the monster's grasp was on her neck.

I lifted my face to cry out—and at the open window I saw that hideous and hated face! He grinned. I rushed towards the window. I drew a pistol from my pocket and fired, but he escaped. He ran with the swiftness of lightning and plunged into the lake.

The crack of the pistol brought a crowd into the room. I pointed to the spot where the murderer had disappeared. We followed the track with boats. Nets were cast, but we found nothing. The other guests searched the countryside.

I was lost in a cloud of wonder and horror. I had survived the death of William, the execution of Justine, the murder of Henry, and now my wife. My father even now might be in his grasp. Ernest might be dead at his feet. This thought called me to action.

I returned to Geneva immediately. My father and Ernest were alive, but my father sank under the news I brought. His eyes lost their shine. He had lost his darling Elizabeth whom he had loved like a daughter. He could not live under the horrors that surrounded him, and gave up all hope of living. He was unable to rise from his bed, and in a few days he died in my arms.

What then became of me? I don't know exactly. I passed out, and chains and darkness were the only things that pressed upon me. Sometimes I dreamed that I wandered in flowery meadows with my old school friends. But I awoke and found myself in a kind of dungeon. Slowly I came to my senses, and was told what had happened. I had been declared insane. For months I had lived in this cell—alone—raving with madness.

I was set free. And I had awakened with a thirst for revenge. I could not control the rage that filled my soul when I thought of the monster I had brought into this world. I prayed to God that I would find the fiend and destroy him. I would follow him over mountains, or forests, or even across a sea of ice. I would search every cave and den. I would go where no man dared to travel. From that moment, I devoted my life to his destruction.

CHAPTER NINETEEN

The Chase

I decided to leave Geneva forever. I took with me a sum of money and some of my mother's jewels. Before I left the town, I went to the cemetery where William, Elizabeth, and my father were buried.

My grief quickly turned to rage. They were dead, and I lived. I wanted to die, too—but their murderer also lived. I knelt on the grass and kissed the earth. I exclaimed, "O ghosts of my loved ones! I vow to pursue the demon who caused this misery until he or I dies. I will not die. I will live to find him. Let the cursed and horrible monster drink deep of agony."

I was answered by a loud and terrible laugh. It rang on my ears long and heavily. And then a well-known voice spoke to me in a whisper. "I am satisfied, miserable creature! You have decided to live, and I am satisfied."

I darted towards the spot from which the sound came, but the devil escaped my grasp. Just then, the bright moon rose and shone full upon his ghastly and distorted shape. He fled with inhuman speed.

And now my wanderings began. They will cease only with death. I have been over much of the earth. I have prayed for death many times. But revenge kept me alive. I dared not die and leave my enemy alive.

And so I chased the monster. Guided by a small clue, I followed the Rhone River and came to the blue Mediterranean Sea. By a strange chance I saw the monster hide himself on a ship bound for the Black Sea. I boarded the same ship. I do not know how he escaped.

It was only during sleep that I could taste joy. O blessed sleep! It was my only time of hope. In sleep I could dream and see my friends, my wife, and my beloved country.

I followed his track through Turkey and Russia. Sometimes the peasants I met helped me follow his path. Sometimes he left some mark to guide me. When the snows came, I saw the print of his huge step on the white field.

Sometimes he left writings on tree bark or cut in stone. Once he wrote, "Follow me. I seek the everlasting ices of the north. There you will feel the misery of cold and frost. You will find near this place a dead rabbit, which I left for you to eat. Come on, my enemy. We have yet to wrestle for our lives."

The snows thickened and the cold increased. It was almost too much for me to bear. The rivers were covered with ice, and food was scarce. The monster left me another message. "Prepare! Your hardships only begin. Wrap yourself in furs and pack food."

Finally the frozen Arctic Ocean appeared at a distance on the horizon. Some weeks before, I had obtained a sled and dogs. This allowed me to speed across the snows, and I gained on the creature. When I first saw the ocean, he was only one day's journey ahead. I hoped to catch him before he reached the shore.

In two days I arrived at a village on the sea-shore. I was told that a gigantic monster had arrived the night before, armed with pistols. He had carried off a family's supply of winter food, and stolen a sled with many dogs. That same night he had gone out across the sea—in a direction that led to no land. I bought a new sled and dogs, and followed him.

I cannot guess how many days have now passed since then. By the amount of supplies I used, I would guess that three weeks have gone by. Gigantic mountains of ice often blocked my way. The ice would often split apart, and I would drift helplessly on the sea. But then the frosts would come and make the paths of the sea safe again.

Once, the poor dogs had reached the top of an ice mountain. It had been terribly hard work. One of the dogs died. I had lost almost all hope. And then suddenly I saw a dark speck on the ice. I saw a sled and the distorted figure of the creature. I wept aloud.

But then the ice split and cracked with a tremendous sound. In a few minutes a dangerous sea rolled between me and my enemy. I was left drifting on a scattered piece of ice.

Many hours passed. Several of my dogs died. I felt myself about to die. And then I saw your ship, Captain Walton. I had no idea that ships ever came so far north. I quickly destroyed part of my sled to construct oars. I decided that if you were going southward, I would ask you to give me a boat. I had to keep chasing the monster. But I was in luck and you were going northward.

Oh! When will I be allowed to rest? Or must I die and the monster still live?

If I do die, swear to me, Walton, that he will not escape. When I am dead, swear that he will not live. He speaks well, and once his words even had power over *my* heart. But don't trust him! His soul is as wicked as his looks. Don't listen to him! Call on the names of William, Justine, Henry, Elizabeth, my father, and of the wretched Victor, and thrust your sword into his heart. My spirit will hover near and direct the steel aright.

CHAPTER TWENTY

Walton's Letters Continued
The End

August 26th

Dear Margaret,

You have read this strange and terrific story of Victor Frankenstein. Do you not feel your blood curdle with horror?

I know the story is true, for I have seen the monster from our ship. The monster exists!

A week has passed while I have listened to this strange tale. What a great man Frankenstein must have been. Even now he seems noble and godlike! Must I lose this wonderful man? I longed for a friend. Have I gained him only to lose him?

He is indeed a great man with great ideas. Yet he sees his life as over—except for this last cause. I have tried to convince him that his life is worth living, but he rejects my words.

"I thank you, Walton," he said, "for your kindness. But I have lost so much already. I can never replace Elizabeth, or Henry, or my brother, or father. I am not who I once was. I am destroyed. I must destroy the being to whom I gave existence. Then I can die."

September 2nd

My beloved Sister,

I write to you while I am in great danger. I do not know if I will ever see dear England and my dearer friends again.

I am surrounded by mountains of ice which offer no escape. The brave sailors look towards me for aid, but I have none to give. It is terrible to realize that the lives of all these men are in danger because of me. It was I who wanted to take up this adventure. My own dreams of greatness have put us all in danger. If we are lost, my mad schemes are the cause.

September 5th

This morning half a dozen sailors demanded entrance into my cabin. They were afraid that if the ice melted, I would be reckless enough to continue my voyage northward. They insisted that I make a solemn promise to return home if the ship should be freed.

Frankenstein turned to the men. He said, "Are you so easily turned from your task? Did you not call this a glorious expedition? Your names were going to be listed among the brave men who faced death for the benefit of mankind. And now at the first hint of danger you shrink away. Oh! Be men, or be more than men. Do not return to your families in disgrace. Return as heroes who don't turn their backs on the enemy."

As you can imagine, the men listened to these words. I told them to consider what had been said. I would not lead them farther north if they wanted to go home. But I said I hoped their courage would return.

How all this will end, I know not. I would rather die than return shamefully without fulfilling my purpose. Yet, I'm afraid that I will not achieve my dream.

September 7th
It has been decided. I have agreed to return if we are not destroyed in the ice. And so my hopes are crushed by the fear of my men. It is hard for me to bear this failure.

September 12th
It is past. I am returning to England. I have lost my hopes of usefulness and glory. I have lost my friend. But I will try to relate these bitter events to you, my dear sister.

September 9th, the ice began to move. A breeze sprang from the west, and on the 11th the passage towards the south became perfectly free. When the sailors saw this, a shout of joy broke from them. Frankenstein awoke and asked the cause of the commotion. "They shout," I said, "because they will soon return to England."

"Do so if you will," he replied, "but I will not. You may give up your purpose, but mine is assigned to me by heaven, and I dare not. I am weak, but surely the spirits will give me strength."

He tried to spring from the bed, but the effort was too great for him. He fell back and fainted.

It was long before he was recovered. I often thought his life was entirely gone. But then he opened his eyes. He breathed with difficulty and was unable to speak. The surgeon gave him a calming potion and ordered us to leave him alone. The doctor told me that my friend did not have many hours to live.

I sat by his bed, watching him. Presently he called to me in a weak voice. "Alas! The strength I relied on is gone. I feel that I shall soon die, and my enemy may still be alive. As his creator, I was required to make sure he was happy, this is true. But he was evil and selfish. He destroyed my friends. I do not know where his thirst for revenge may end. He should die. It was my task to destroy him, but I have failed. I asked you to complete my work. I ask you again now.

"Farewell, Walton! Avoid ambition, even if it is only trying to make a name for yourself in science and discoveries. Yet, why do I say this? I have lost all hope, yet another may succeed...."

His voice became fainter as he spoke. He pressed my hand weakly. Then his eyes closed forever, while the shadow of a gentle smile passed away from his lips.

Margaret, what can I say that will allow you to understand my sorrow? My tears flow. My mind is clouded by disappointment. But I journey towards England, and I may find comfort there.

I am interrupted. What do these sounds mean? It is midnight. The breeze blows fairly. Again there is a sound of a human voice, but hoarser. It comes from the cabin where the remains of Frankenstein still lie. I must arise and examine. Good night, my sister.

Great God! What a scene has just taken place! I am still dizzy just thinking of it! I hardly know whether I shall have the power to explain it.

I entered the cabin. Over the body of Frankenstein hung a form which I cannot find words to describe. It was gigantic and tall, but it looked awkward and distorted. His face was hidden by long locks of ragged hair. He held out one immense, mummy-like hand. When he heard me coming into the cabin, he sprang towards the window.

Never did I behold a vision so horrible as his face. I shut my eyes and called on him to stay.

He paused, looking at me with wonder. Then he turned back to the lifeless form of his creator.

"That is also my victim!" he exclaimed. "In his murder my crimes are finished. Oh, Frankenstein! What does it help that I now ask you to forgive me? I destroyed you by destroying all you loved. Alas! He is cold, he cannot answer me."

I approached this tremendous being. He was so frightening and ugly that I dared not again raise my eyes to his face. I gathered strength to speak.

"It does no good," I said, "to say regrets now. If you had listened to your heart before, Frankenstein would have lived."

"Ha! You're dreaming!" cried the demon. "You think I never listened to my heart? I *tried* to love. I suffered terribly when I was turned to hatred and wickedness. You cannot imagine the pain. Ah, but now it is ended. There is my last victim!"

"Monster!" I said. "You only mourn because the victim of your hate is gone. You have no more power over him."

"Oh, it is not so," he said. "I mourn because he will never know my misery. I did destroy his hopes, but this brought me no joy. I wished for love and friendship, but I was hated. Where is the justice in that? Am I the only criminal in all this? Why do you not hate Felix, who drove me from his door? Why do you not curse the man who shot me after I saved his child? No, *they* are noble and flawless beings! *I* am a monster to be despised, and kicked, and trampled on.

"You hate me," he went on, "but I hate myself even more. And now, the only death I seek is my own. I will leave your ship and find the most northern place on the globe. I will burn this miserable body of mine. I will die. Where can I find rest but in death?

"Farewell!" he cried. "I leave you. You are the last human I will ever see. Farewell, Frankenstein! Soon I shall die. I shall climb onto my funeral pile and rejoice in the flames. The light of that blaze will fade away. My ashes will be swept into the sea. My spirit will sleep in peace. Farewell."

He sprang from the cabin window as he said this. He landed on the ice raft which lay close to the ship. He was soon borne away by the waves and lost in darkness and distance.

MARY SHELLEY

Mary Wollstonecraft Shelley was only nineteen when she started writing her masterpiece—*Frankenstein*. She was born in London, England, in 1797 to William Godwin, a noted philosopher, and Mary Wollstonecraft, a respected female writer. Her mother died soon after young Mary was born. Mary was raised by a stepmother and her father. Her father had many famous writers and thinkers as friends, who influenced Mary as she was growing up.

At nineteen, Mary was with her husband, the poet Percy Bysshe Shelley, and a group of fellow writers in Switzerland. They decided to hold a writing contest. Each was to come up with a frightening tale. Thus, *Frankenstein* was born. Her friends applauded her work, and her tale of horror and "human" nature was published in 1818.

Mary had four children, but the first three died by the time Mary was 22. Tragically, her husband died in a drowning accident a few years later. Mary Shelley wrote other works throughout her life, but *Frankenstein* remained her most famous novel. She died in 1851.